THE WINGED-SERPENT PRINCESS

RAY THORNE

Dedicated to the love of my life—

You always help inspire me to keep going
with your beautiful encouragement and
constant patience with all things creative and
real. You are my world.

The afternoon sunlight shone down on the fields that surrounded King Shepperton's castle. The king's daughter, Princess Audrelle, peered out the window of her bedroom, smelled the cool spring air, and decided to go out into the fields to pick berries. After hurriedly combing a few tangles out of her golden-blond hair, she gathered up her shawl and berry-picking basket and walked toward the door to go out. King Shepperton walked into the hall and noticed his daughter opening the door to leave.

"Going out?" he asked Audrelle.

"Yes, Father," replied the princess, planting a kiss on the king's cheek. "I'm going to pick some berries and enjoy some of this nice weather."

"Be careful," said the king. "Enjoy yourself. I shall get my reading done this afternoon."

Audrelle smiled at her father and exited the castle. The king watched as his daughter began to skip gleefully into the fields across the castle moat.

The princess wandered here and there, trying to remember where the best berry bushes were in the forest that surrounded the fields. When she discovered some in a shady clearing, she stopped to do some picking. As she plucked the larger berries from the bushes and placed them into her basket, she noticed that the chirping of the birds in the trees had suddenly stopped.

Audrelle looked up. A strange feeling came over her. As she looked around her, the forest grew more and more silent with every second and the sky grew darker and darker as clouds grew thicker in the sky. "It didn't look like rain was on the way," whispered Audrelle to herself. "What's going on?"

She went back to picking, but faster this time because she didn't want to get caught in the rain should it start to pour down. The forest remained dead silent as an eerie fog began to settle in the trees. Audrelle grew more anxious, so she decided to head back to the safety of the castle. Looking down at her half-full basket of berries, she sighed in annoyance at the sudden change in the weather.

Audrelle walked briskly onward toward the field leading back home. Suddenly, an unearthly shriek shattered the silence and the ground beneath her feet began to tremble. Audrelle gasped in fear. Then, before her, the ground began to break open in several places, and an ungodly sight met her eyes. From the tears in the earth, ten rotting corpses arose. The corpses had blackened, dried flesh hanging off their bones. They wore rusty armor, and on their shields and swords was the coat of arms of her father's long-quieted enemy. When Audrelle was a little girl, King Shepperton and his men had battled and defeated this kingdom due to its attempts to use black magic and sorcery to take over his kingdom.

Audrelle trembled as she watched the corpses grind their rotten teeth while they stepped toward her with their swords leveled at her. The princess screamed, turned, and ran from them. The corpses shrieked again and sprinted after her, their armor clanking against their skeletons. As she ran, Audrelle tried to comprehend what she was witnessing. All she could figure out was that this was some form of the sorcery her father had talked about in the past. She prayed for deliverance as the castle came into view in the distance.

Something massive landed in front of her. It appeared to have come from the sky. Dirt sprayed up into a cloud of dust as the princess stumbled at the sudden jolt and landed face-first in the field. She moaned in pain and slowly looked up to see what it was that had landed in front of her. What she saw was even more terrifying to her than the corpse army that was pursuing her. It was Gorgomesh the dragon, with his shimmering, black scaly body and enormous wingspan that stretched toward the heavens.

Gorgomesh's nostrils flared, and his red eyes, glowing with hatred, pierced Audrelle's. The beast arose, standing at a height of about thirty feet, and glared down again at the woman kneeling before him. Audrelle looked up into the glowing eyes of the creature and tried to scream but found that she could not.

The corpse army arrived at Audrelle's side and grabbed her by both her arms. They stood her up before Gorgomesh.

From behind the body of the great beast stepped a tall figure wearing a long, black hooded cloak. His face was hidden beneath his hood. It was the evil wizard king Merlot. He walked forward and stood before Audrelle. He raised his bony white hand to the princess's chin and turned her fear-filled face toward his.

"It's been a long time." Merlot spoke in a voice that hardly rose above a whisper. "Now my destiny is almost complete."

Audrelle's lip quivered as tears began to stream down her cheeks. "Let me go!" she lamented. "What do you want of me?"

"Much," answered Merlot. "With your sudden absence, your father will have no choice but to surrender his kingdom unto me. Take her to my castle!"

The corpse army let go of Audrelle's arms as Gorgomesh raised his massive claw toward the princess. The beast picked up Audrelle despite her attempts to squirm away. Gorgomesh spread his wings and, in an instant, shot into the air with tremendous force. The corpse army and Merlot stood watching Gorgomesh as he carried the princess away into the skies.

Merlot turned to the army and raised his hand toward them. "Come with me," he ordered as an electrifying blast shot out of his finger, causing the army to disappear into thin air along with Merlot himself.

Marquis Orlock stood on the bow of his ship. He had dark eyes, and his long, black hair blew in the sea breeze. He and his crew had been at sea for several months now, and the crew was beginning to grow weary from the journey. Orlock's first mate, Raban, walked from the stern to the bow and stood beside him.

"Captain Orlock, the men are growing even wearier," said Raban. "When will we reach a port?"

"Soon," replied Orlock. "I can feel it in the air. The smell of the sea breeze beckons us closer and closer."

"But the island we are headed toward is uncharted," continued Raban, "and heaven only knows if we will actually find it."

"Do not doubt the vision I had," retorted Orlock. "The images I saw coincided with the map I found on that trip to the Bermuda Triangle. The spot of land we found there, where the map lay, was uncharted as well. There are many things yet to be discovered on our planet."

"I believe you, Captain." Raban sighed. "When or if we get to the destination, what will we discover there?"

"An oracle of all knowledge resides there," replied Orlock. "In my vision I saw a woman and the oracle. The oracle was beckoning for me to follow it and said that the woman was in jeopardy. I must find out what this all means. Therefore, we must find that island."

"Yes, Captain," said Raban. He bowed and turned to leave Orlock's side. "I will notify the men that we must sail a bit longer and that we are getting closer."

Marquis Orlock nodded at the first mate. "Yes," he said sternly. "Tell them we are getting close."

After Raban had disappeared below deck to talk to the crew members, Orlock stood motionless for a moment in thought. He sighed as he reached for the rolled-up piece of parchment paper in his overcoat. He spread open the parchment—the map he had found in the Bermuda Triangle.

Orlock studied the map. According to the map, they should have reached their destination the day before. He wondered whether they would find the island at any moment—if it was actually there. He fought the temptation to give up and let the voyage be considered a failed attempt. He shook the thought out of his head and put the map back into his pocket.

Orlock strode across the deck to the stern. He had been there for about thirty minutes when the mate, standing in the crow's nest, began to shout. Orlock looked up at the crew member and saw him pointing toward the horizon, where the ship's bow was directed In the distance, a great cloud of fog rested on the water. It was thick and dark gray.

Orlock rushed to the bow and stared intently at the fog. "We must be close," he said to himself. "The map showed the drawing of the island, and it was shrouded in a dense fog."

After calling the crew members to the deck, Orlock took the helm of the ship and steered it into the fog.

"Is this the fog that is on the map?" asked Raban as he arrived at Orlock's side.

"It must be," replied Orlock. "We should have reached the island yesterday. I figured something like this would happen. The map was somewhat crudely drawn anyway—the cartographer could have made an error."

Raban, who had been staring intently at the cloud of fog, relaxed. "I'll place men at all four points on the ship and have them watch for any reefs, should we be getting close to land," he said.

"Good idea," agreed Orlock. "We don't want to run aground on the rocks . . . if there are any."

The ship slowly sailed into the fog. The crew members stood peering over the sides of the ship into the black water below. An eerie silence filled the air since the water beneath the cloud didn't contain even a ripple. Orlock had some of the crew furl the sail to improve visibility and avoid any sudden gusts of wind.

"I think I can hear water lapping against a shore, up ahead," whispered Orlock to Raban.

The first mate laid his hand firmly on the captain's shoulder. "I think I can hear it as well," he agreed. "Should I order the men to begin dropping the sounding line?"

"Yes, Raban," answered Orlock.

A crew member dropped the sounding line. "Five fathoms!" he called out to the captain.

"Be ready to cast the anchor!" ordered Orlock.

The men made ready the anchor at the bow of the ship and waited for the captain's orders to drop. Orlock peered hard into the cloud before them. After a moment of silence, the silhouette of land masses appeared in the distance. "Drop anchor!" he ordered.

The crew members let the anchor fall from the side of the ship. The craft began to lurch as the anchor dragged along the ocean floor. The anchor finally brought the ship to a wobbling standstill.

Everyone on the ship breathed hard in the silence as they stared at the tall rock formations that stood on the land ahead of them.

"It's actually here," muttered Raban to Orlock. "The map told us the truth. Your vision is coming to fruition, Captain."

"Yes, Raban," said Orlock, a small grin crossing his lips. "I am glad none of this was in vain."

Princess Audrelle slowly opened her eyes. She awoke with her cheek pressed against the cold, wet stone floor of Merlot's prison chamber. She had fainted during the flight to the wizard king's decrepit castle, which sat on an island, atop a foothill amid dark mountains.

The island's inhabitants lived in a village on the opposite side of the island. They kept to themselves to avoid drawing Merlot's attention. They knew there was some sort of agreement between the king and Gorgomesh the dragon, and they knew their village would be destroyed if they did anything to displease the king. Audrelle had known about all this for some time, since her father had told her stories of the evil wizard and she had read books from her father's library.

Audrelle shakily rose to her feet and peered around the dark, cold chamber. She noticed a door across the room. She tried to open it but to no avail. She called out for help through the barred window at the top of the heavy door.

A large guard appeared at the window. He too was part of Merlot's corpse army. His face was an exposed skull with one rotting eyeball sitting in a socket. "What do you want?" he asked with a grunt. Worms slithered inside the pupil of his eye.

Audrelle tried not to be sick as she looked at the guard. "Please," she pleaded, her voice shaking. "Please let me go! I promise I won't say anything. I want to go home!"

"Merlot will see you in his throne room shortly," said the guard. "He wanted to wait until you came to, so he placed you in this prison chamber in case you awoke and tried to escape."

"I will see the king now," said Audrelle. "If he will see me, that is."

The guard walked away from the door. Audrelle stood silently as she watched him go down the prison hallway and out of sight. She remained at the door for what seemed like a long time before the guard returned. He took a set of keys from his armor belt and opened the door.

The guard pulled his sword from its sheath and pointed it in Audrelle's direction. "Follow me," he ordered. "And don't try anything, like running, because there is no escaping this castle!"

Audrelle nervously acknowledged his order. She walked alongside the guard, who kept his sword pointed at her side. They walked down a long corridor and into the wizard king's main chamber, where he sat on a black metal throne.

Audrelle gulped at the sight of the hooded figure sitting in the wicked-looking chair, lightly tapping his bony fingers on the armrests. The guard nudged the princess forward, closer to Merlot, where she stood speechless.

"I'm glad you have come to my kingdom," hissed the king from beneath the shroud of his hood. "I assume your accommodations were not satisfactory?"

Audrelle tried to answer him, but nothing could pass from her lips.

"Speak up, young woman!" snarled Merlot.

"I-I'm sorry," stammered Audrelle. "I-I am not used to sleeping on a cold stone floor."

"I figured as much," said Merlot. "I will see to it that you have more comfortable accommodations. I just needed to prepare your chamber upon your arrival."

"How long will I have to stay here?" whimpered Audrelle.

"That will depend on your father," replied Merlot. "Whether he will hand his kingdom over to me willingly or not. Last time it was not so willingly, but I imagine, with the kidnapping of his only child, he will think twice this time."

Audrelle started to feel the burn of tears in her eyes. "Why must you persist in doing this? Why can't you just leave us alone?"

"It's a simple answer, darling," answered Merlot. "Power ... absolute power. I now have an ally in Gorgomesh the dragon. He has agreed to join me in my conquest and will share in the prize. Together we will bring our powers to the ultimate heights, and the world will fall at our feet in return."

Audrelle stood stunned as she looked up at Merlot. Her eyes grew wide in fear as what he had to say sank into her mind. "I don't know what to say," she stammered. Desperate rage began to grow inside her. "Other than, you might as well kill me now!"

Merlot looked up from under his hood, revealing a flash of bony white face and blackened teeth. "Why would I do that now?" he asked, perplexed at the sudden change in the princess's tone.

"Because," said Audrelle as the burning anger grew inside her, "I would rather die than let a disgusting thing like you take over my father's kingdom! He will send you all to the deepest reaches of hell before you can blink twice!"

Merlot stood up, enraged. He lifted his hand and a glowing green bolt of lightning shot from his fingertips. The bolt struck Audrelle in the stomach, and she fell to her knees in anguish.

"Stupid girl," Merlot snarled. He looked from the kneeling princess to the guard standing behind her. "Take the princess to the chamber I've prepared for her and lock the door! I've had enough of her insolence for one day."

The guard walked up to the princess and placed his hand on her shoulder. Audrelle, despite the pain in her stomach, managed to pull herself together and stand up abruptly. She spit in the direction of Merlot, then reeled around and swung her arm at the guard's face. The blow sent the guard stumbling backward as Audrelle sprinted toward the chamber door.

"After the imbecile!" yelled Merlot, shooting another lightning bolt from his fingertip.

The bolt whizzed past Audrelle's head and struck the doorpost as she exited the chamber. The princess was determined to escape. She looked around for another door. At the end of the hall outside Merlot's throne chamber, she found a small door off to the side. She opened the door and saw a crawl space. Figuring that this was a better spot to hide than out in the open in the hall, she knelt down and quickly wedged herself into the space.

After shutting the door behind her, Audrelle assessed her surroundings. The crawl space was pitch dark inside and only large enough for her to stay on her hands and knees. She blindly felt into the darkness in front of her and discovered that the space kept going for another several feet. Audrelle continued to move, blinded by the darkness, until she finally reached the end of the crawl space. "I must be at least ten feet from the door," she whispered to herself. "I don't know how long I will be able to stay hidden in here, but this is better than nothing."

As her eyes began to adjust to the darkness, Audrelle noticed that the crawl space opened up into a small tunnel to the right. At the end of the tunnel, she saw what looked like a glowing orange light. "A light?" she asked herself. "Maybe it's a way out? Maybe it's a way outside the castle?"

Audrelle sighed and decided to squeeze herself into the stone tunnel. She barely fit. With a lot of painful squirming against the stone floor to get to the glowing light ahead, she managed to reach the end of the tunnel. The light came from a huge dungeon deep within the castle.

Audrelle popped her head out of the tunnel opening, which was set in the dungeon wall about six feet off the ground. As she scanned the dungeon to see if anyone was present, she noticed a set of wooden tables with a lot of bottles and instruments on them at the center of the room. She didn't see anyone around, so she pulled herself out of the opening and dropped to the floor.

"So what does Merlot have going on in here?" asked Audrelle, walking up to one of the tables and lifting a bottle from it. She gazed at the bottle, which contained a liquid that gave off a weird glow. She pursed her lips in curiosity as she put the bottle back down and looked around at the other tables. "I wonder what these are for?" she asked herself, moving to another table and inspecting its contents.

Curiosity overtook Audrelle. She became preoccupied with the room and forgot that she was on the run from Merlot and his men. As she stood there looking at the instruments and other weird items on the tables, which she concluded were part of his sorcery, Audrelle noticed a hole in the floor off to one side of the dungeon. The hole gave off intermittent flashes of green, glowing light, which was accompanied by mist that swirled around and disappeared into the air above.

When the light reached Audrelle's eyes, she quickly covered her face as a sudden fear came over her. "What was that?" she whispered. She rubbed her eyes, confused at her sudden fear. She looked back toward the hole, wanting to investigate what was in there. Another flash of green light appeared, and the mist clouded upward.

Audrelle stood stunned and in awe at the sight. She felt all her emotions go strangely numb. Then her body became numb—she felt nothing at all—as she began to take small steps toward the hole. Closer and closer Audrelle stepped toward the sight, as if in a trance. In the back of her mind, she knew she needed to run as far from that hole as she could, but her body refused to cooperate. When her toes reached the edge of it, Audrelle peered down as the light and mist swirled around, making the hole look like some magical well.

Audrelle knelt beside the edge of the hole and moved her face closer to the light. In the hole, at what appeared to be the bottom, lay a coiled serpent. It was hissing at Audrelle. She became transfixed on the creature as it began to swim, a ghostly shimmer emanated within the mist and light that surrounded it. The serpent's tongue flicked in and out of its mouth while its eyes glowed with a bright, white light.

Audrelle felt a surge of fear shoot up her spine, and she gasped as her mind and body seemed to break free from the trance she was in. The serpent locked eyes with her and, in an instant, leapt from the hole. Its body disappeared, like a flash of lightning, into her face. Audrelle stumbled backward from the sudden attack and fell onto her back.

The princess lay shaking on the dungeon floor in shock and horror as surges of glowing energy traveled in and out of her body and disappeared within her skin. At first she felt agony and fear, but it subsided as she felt her mind go blank and she lapsed into unconsciousness.

Marquis Orlock, Raban, and three crew members loaded themselves into a skiff and rowed across the black, fog-shrouded water toward the beach.

"According to the map," said Orlock, "we will land on a beach with a nearby cave. We need to avoid the cave at all costs."

"Why is that, Captain?" asked Raban.

"I am not completely certain," replied Orlock. "But I believe this island may contain things that man should not see or be within the vicinity of. After all, the island already contains the cave in which the oracle dwells. So who knows what other things we may come across?"

The men in the skiff nodded in understanding but couldn't help shivering in fear at the thought of the possible dangers. Marquis Orlock tried to maintain his calm demeanor and stared coldly at the beach as it neared. When the skiff reached the rocky shore of the stone-covered beach, the five men hopped onto the dry land.

"All right, men, follow me," said Orlock. "Whatever you do, always be aware of your surroundings."

The five men started to trudge over the rocks. The stony terrain began turning into sand the farther they went. Raban placed his hand on Orlock's shoulder as they approached some rock formations.

"What is it?" asked Orlock.

"There, Captain," replied the first mate, pointing at a large cave in the distance.

"The map is proving correct," exclaimed the captain. "This is wonderful news! We shall find the oracle in no time."

They continued onward across the sand until they were several yards from the cave, where Orlock warned the men to remain as quiet as possible. The sound of an animal grunting emanated from the darkness of the mouth of the cave. "Remain still, men," ordered Orlock in a whisper. "Let's see what happens."

The cave fell quiet. Not a sound could be heard around the men now. It seemed that any life around them had gone into hiding. Orlock stared bullets into the dark mouth of the cave, and his brow furrowed in anticipation. Dead silence hung in the air. Orlock slowly waved the men forward with him.

An unearthly roar broke the silence and echoed across the terrain, sending the five men to their knees in fright. From out of the blackness of the cave came a beast. It stood over fifteen feet in height and had the head, arms, and torso of a gorilla, reptilian legs and feet, and two large ram's horns growing from the top of its head. But what frightened the men the most was the large, single eye beneath its fierce brow.

"The cyclops," muttered Orlock.

"The creature of the legends," whimpered Raban.

The other three men simply shook, still kneeling, and gazed at the creature in fear-filled awe.

The beast looked around the sandy terrain, sniffed the air, and let out another roar while beating its chest. At the echoing sound, the men covered their ears in terror.

"I don't think it saw us," whispered Orlock. "The creature has limited vision. But who knows what natural instincts it might have?"

Orlock and the men slowly rose to their feet and watched as the cyclops searched the area around the cave. It felt like an eternity to the men before the beast stopped, grunted, and walked back into the cave. With as much determination as they could muster, Orlock and the men moved as quickly as possible past the cave and onward toward their destination.

A few hours passed before the five men decided to rest. The mountainous terrain in which they had been traveling for a while had taken a toll on their feet, and to continue onward to the cave of the oracle they needed sustenance. Orlock kindly gave the others food rations and took a smaller portion for himself.

"Captain?" asked Raban. "Why do you not take for yourself a portion the size of ours?"

Orlock sat silent for a moment. "I want to make sure you men have plenty to eat," he said quietly. "After all, this is a voyage in which I've brought you all into danger."

"We are with you, Captain, all the way," said Raban while the other three men grunted in agreement.

Marquis Orlock smiled at the men in appreciation. Raban eyed the captain, who slyly took his small food ration and placed it back in the travel bag. They continued to rest for a little while longer, then started again on their trek.

When they had gone about a mile, Raban ran up to Orlock, who was leading by a couple of yards. "Captain," started Raban. He glanced behind him to be certain that he was out of earshot of the other men. "Why did you not eat?"

"What do you mean?" asked Orlock.

"I saw you put your ration back in the bag," continued Raban. "You will die if you don't eat."

"Don't worry yourself over me," said Orlock. "I know when I need to eat."

Raban looked at the captain suspiciously. "Please, Captain," he said. "I will keep my concerns to myself, but please tell me if you are ill or need anything."

"Thank you, my good man," smiled Orlock, placing a hand on Raban's shoulder. "You're indispensable to me and our journeys together."

The sun had reached the middle of the sky overhead when the travelers reached the cave that supposedly contained the oracle of all knowledge. Orlock looked upon the entrance of the cave and saw markings inscribed by some ancient civilization. He tried to read it but could not make out any of the markings.

"According to the map, this is it," said Orlock to the others. "This is the cave we seek."

The men entered the cave and saw that it led far into the mountainside. They lit a couple of small torches they had brought with them in the travel bag. The walls of the tunnel dripped with a damp ooze, and more encryptions were visible to the men as they walked. The torches flicked eerie blobs of light into the blackness that went before them. Eventually the tunnel ended in a massive cavern.

Enormous stalactites covered the ceiling of the cavern, creating an underground cathedral of dark beauty. A ridge ran along the edge of the cavern, carved out by people thousands of years before, which led to the cavern base. At the center of the cavern base was a large stone well with more inscriptions on the surfaces of its edges.

Orlock and the men carefully walked down the ridge to the base. "Be careful not to make much noise," whispered Orlock to the others.

"We don't want to cause any of those stalactites to fall on us like an avalanche."

"Given their size," added Raban, "they must be thousands of years old. I wouldn't doubt some of them are ready to crack at any moment."

"Truth," said Orlock. "It's very dry in here. The stalactites were created by water dripping from the top of the cavern and mixing with the minerals in the rock. Given the dryness of the cavern, there probably hasn't been any water runoff or seepage down here in hundreds of years."

The five men cautiously walked up to the well, and Orlock placed his hand on the inscriptions, running his finger across the surface of their carved edges.

"How is the oracle summoned?" asked Raban, eyeing Orlock.

"I believe that if I am able to read these inscriptions aloud," replied Orlock, "it should summon it."

Orlock did his best to read the letters and symbols in the inscriptions. The other men watched him anxiously. When Orlock reached the end of the inscribed passage, he stood back. A gust of wind suddenly soared up from the well. The five men stood in awe as a yellowish light appeared from the hole and formed itself into an orb, which floated above the well and shimmered before them. Within the orb appeared a figure cloaked in white with its face covered.

The figure removed its facial covering, revealing a foggy black hole with two glowing eyes with cat-like pupils. The five men's mouths dropped open at the sight.

"You summoned me," came a voice from the figure, in a deep whisper.

"Y-yes," replied Orlock, trembling. "I am Marquis Orlock, and I have come to enquire about a vision—"

"I know who you are," interrupted the figure. "I am the oracle, and I know why you have come."

"Then please explain to me my vision," said Orlock.

"There is a princess in deep trouble," said the oracle. "She has been kidnapped by the evil forces of King Merlot, of the forbidden lands of Gorgomesh the dragon. Merlot and Gorgomesh have joined forces in a planned attempt to rule the lands. As of this moment they are successful in their attempt."

"The princess," asked Orlock. "What does she have to do with their plan to take over?"

"She is the daughter of good King Shepperton," answered the oracle. "Princess Audrelle is Merlot's final key to taking over the last kingdom that stands in his way . . . the last kingdom that holds any good left in these lands. That kingdom is under the rule of King Shepperton. Merlot will use taking the princess captive to cripple King Shepperton."

"I understand," said Orlock. "But what do I have to do with any of this?"

"You and your men are the only ones left in the lands who are fearless enough to help the princess," answered the oracle. "It is your destiny, Marquis Orlock. It is your destiny to help save the lands from the evils that prevail in these times."

Orlock sighed and tried not to roll his eyes. "I knew it was going to be something like this," he muttered. "I have my own personal issues to deal with. I don't know that I am capable of undertaking this venture."

"It is your destiny," said the oracle sharply. "The kingdom needs you, the lands need you . . . the princess needs you."

Orlock quickly stood up straight at attention. "Yes, Oracle." He nodded. "I will do my best."

"Now go," ordered the oracle. "Go fulfill your destiny before it is too late!"

"Before we go," said Orlock, "where is all of this taking place? I need coordinates to get there!"

The oracle pointed toward the edge of the well, where a map magically appeared next to the inscriptions. "Your coordinates are there," he said. "May good fortune be with you and your crew!"

With that, the oracle disappeared in a flash of white light that traveled back down into the well, leaving the five men standing there speechless.

Orlock walked up to the well and picked up the map. After putting the map in his pocket, he turned toward the others. "Well, men," he said, "are you with me?"

"Yes, Captain," answered Raban, "to the ends of the earth." The other three men nodded in agreement.

Orlock placed his hand on Raban's shoulder and thanked him and the others before they started the trek back out of the cave. When they reached the top of the opening to the chamber of the oracle, they looked back just as a stalactite fell from the ceiling and crashed to the ground. "We have to get out of here," said Orlock. "This place is beyond dangerous for us. We don't want to end up being buried alive."

The five men briskly but carefully rushed through the cave as more stalactites and rocks began to crumble behind them. The light of the opening to the cave met their eyes and they stepped out into it, sighing with relief. They had made it out just in time to see the cave collapse behind them.

"Good work, men," panted Orlock. He smiled. "We made it!"

A large shadow loomed over the five men. They looked up to see what was causing it and jumped back in fear as the angry eye of the cyclops stared death into their faces. The beast let out a roar and beat its chest before slamming its fist onto the ground next to them.

"Draw your swords!" shouted Orlock. He pulled his sword from its sheath.

The cyclops snarled in defiance at the men as they prepared to defend themselves. The beast swung its massive fist at one of the crew members and sent the poor man flying into the rocks next to the collapsed cave. His body exploded into a red mist upon impact.

Orlock screamed in horror as he watched the man die before his eyes. "You will die for that!" he hissed at the creature. He ran toward it with his sword held high above his head.

Raban rushed to the cyclops's side and drove his sword deep into the creature's reptilian leg. The beast let out a howl and reached for the first mate, but Raban dodged its hand and swung his sword in the process. The blade sliced into the beast's wrist, sending blood spurting into Raban's face.

Orlock and the other two crew members began to attack the creature from the other side while it was preoccupied with its bleeding wrist. The cyclops roared in pain and anger, swinging its good arm at the others, and picked up one of the crewmen. The man swung his sword back and forth at the beast's face, trying to save himself as the cyclops drew him in close to its mouth to crush him in its teeth. Orlock sidestepped and plunged his sword into the creature's stomach.

The cyclops dropped the crewman and fell to its knees. The four men watched the cyclops as it panted and wheezed, with blood gushing out of its stomach and onto the ground beneath it.

"An eye for an eye," murmured Orlock under his breath angrily. The cyclops slowly looked up at Orlock, its eye glaring but its lips beginning to tremble. Orlock glared back at the creature.

The cyclops grunted, then quietly sat looking at all the men for a moment before its pupil grew wide as life began to leave it. The beast fell limp onto its side in a pool of blood and let out one last exhale.

"It's dead," said Orlock to the men. "Let's get back to the ship."

They all sheathed their swords, slung their travel bags over their shoulders and turned to leave the site of the fallen cyclops. Orlock stopped and ran back over to the spot where the crewman was killed. He found the man's sword lying on the ground and picked it up, tears welling in his eyes. He quickly wiped the tears from his eyes in an attempt to hide his emotions from the others as he turned back to join them.

"Our man will not be forgotten," said Orlock to the men as they walked. "We will hold a funeral service for him once we get back to the ship."

Audrelle awoke surrounded by curtains. She sat up and realized that she was in a bed. "Oh no," she murmured while rubbing her face. "This isn't where I was when I fainted."

"No, it is not," came Merlot's voice from somewhere on the other side of the bed curtains.

Audrelle quickly opened and peeked out of the curtains, eyeing King Merlot as he strode into the chamber.

"You insolent fool," continued Merlot. He touched his bony hand to his forehead in annoyance.

"Where am I?" asked Audrelle.

"You're in your chamber, princess," replied Merlot. "You fainted in the secret chamber in which I perform my spells and experiments. Where is the serpent?"

Audrelle looked at him, fearfully at first but then questioningly. "Serpent?" she asked, confused.

"You don't remember?" snarled Merlot. "Don't be foolish. Where is the serpent I kept contained in the well in my spell chamber? It was nowhere to be found when I found you in there!"

"I don't remember," answered Audrelle in a whimper. "I don't know what you are talking about!"

Merlot began to grind his teeth in frustration, but then suddenly stopped. His eyes widened. "It is no longer in there," he said to himself while Audrelle looked on quizzically. "It's in her!"

"What do you mean?" asked Audrelle, her voice becoming frantic.

"The prophecy of the winged serpent is coming to pass," continued Merlot to himself. "She must be the chosen one."

"Please, king!" exclaimed Audrelle. "Please tell me what you're talking about!"

"That serpent in my spell chamber," answered Merlot angrily, "was the spirit of the winged serpent of the legends! I have managed to hold it captive for many years. According to an ancient prophecy, it will one day help determine the balance between good and evil when they come together to do battle. It holds extreme power on both sides of the coin! If evil triumphs over good, then evil will rule the lands . . . and if good triumphs over evil, then good will rule the lands! You, my dear princess, are the keeper of this amazing power now."

Audrelle, trembling in fear and confusion, backed up into the bed and away from Merlot as he walked up to its side. "I cannot let good triumph," he continued as a sly grin crossed his lips. "Therefore, you will need to be in alliance with me from now on. Otherwise the plans for my destiny and ever-growing kingdom will crumble."

"I will never join you!" shouted Audrelle defiantly. "You cannot make me. No matter what you do!"

"You will go through changes," said Merlot, laying a hand on the princess's shoulder. "When the full moon rises, the winged serpent will rise from the depths of its slumber."

"I don't understand," whimpered Audrelle.

"You will," said Merlot. "The moon will be full tonight, as a matter of fact, so you will need to come with me."

"Go with you where?" asked Audrelle, tears beginning to stream down her cheeks.

"I have a place to keep you during the full moon," replied Merlot.

The evil king snapped his fingers, and a corpse guard entered the chamber. Merlot pointed to Audrelle, and the guard walked up to the bed. Merlot ordered the princess to stand, so she did. The guard placed shackles on her wrists and guided her out of the room while Merlot led the way.

They exited through the front door of the castle and out into the dreary afternoon light. The clouds were thick and dark gray, and Audrelle shivered as she walked with Merlot and the guard toward a rocky trail. The trail led down the hill from the castle and out to the beach, where the ocean splashed onto the shore.

"This way," ordered Merlot as he pointed to a cave at the bottom of the foothill and just off the beach. They walked across the beach toward the cave. The brisk ocean breeze blew Audrelle's golden hair across her face, and she used it to hide the fear raging inside her. She began to feel there was something severely wrong going on within her, but she could not pinpoint what it was. She wanted to be home with her father and in his kingdom more than anything now, and quietly prayed for deliverance.

When the three figures reached the opening of the cave, Audrelle turned her face toward the ocean. "Please," she whispered, speaking to the horizon as if someone out there could hear her. "Please help me."

The corpse guard pushed her forward into the cave while Merlot pointed them toward chains embedded in a rock wall. The guard pressed the princess up against the wall while Merlot removed the shackles on her wrists and replaced them with shackles attached to the chains in the wall.

"You'll sleep here tonight, princess," said Merlot. "It's not the best of accommodations, but it is the only place that will work while the full moon is high in the sky."

"Please," whimpered Audrelle, "please don't leave me in here!"

Merlot turned from Audrelle and pointed at the guard to leave. "We will be back in the morning, princess," he said seriously. "Pleasant dreams."

They walked away and left Audrelle chained to the cave wall, where she watched them disappear onto the beach and out of sight. After pulling on the chains shackled to her wrists, Audrelle sank to her knees and began to weep convulsively.

Marquis Orlock sat down at his desk in the captain's cabin and sighed. The memorial service for the deceased crewman came to a close. The rest of the crew went back to their duties on the ship as the evening sun began to set over the quiet sea.

As Orlock sat in the silence of his cabin, he heard a knock on the door. "Come in," he said.

Raban slowly poked his head into the door opening. "Captain," the first mate said, "may I speak to you for a moment?"

"Of course," answered Orlock. "Please, do come in."

Raban walked up to the captain's desk and placed his fingers on the sextant that lay on it.

"What is it you wish to speak to me about?" asked Orlock.

"Captain," started Raban, "I am sorry for the loss of the crewman. I know you are upset about it. There is also a storm coming toward us from afar, so I will need to get my orders from you for the men. But I also need to know something . . ."

"And what is that?" asked Orlock.

"I need to know that you are all right," continued Raban. "I have not seen you eat anything this entire voyage, and your skin has grown paler by the day. I understand that you have private issues that you don't wish to discuss, but as your right-hand man, I need to know what's going on with you."

Orlock smiled at the first mate. "I might as well tell you," he said. "But you must swear to me, my good man, that you will not breathe a word to anyone. I will merely let you know so you will stop being concerned about me."

"Mum's the word," said Raban with a nod.

"In short," said Orlock, "I am a vampire."

Raban's eyes widened upon hearing this.

"Do not be afraid," continued Orlock. "I have been cursed by it since birth, but it was not until I reached my early twenties that the curse began to settle in.”

Raban slowly sat down in the chair across from the desk, listening to the captain attentively.

“My mother, Mircalla Orlock, was of good family,” explained Orlock. “She had been taken advantage of by a stranger when she was traveling between the lands of the old country. I was the result of that terrible situation.

“After the attack, she was taken in by a group of nuns in a convent nearby. That convent is where I was born and where the two of us were taken care of by the nuns. As time passed, my mother slowly began to transform into a vampire. Apparently, that was another result of her attack. The stranger who attacked her, it had come to be known, was a vampire.

“The nuns understood this and did what they could to protect the both of us from the townspeople, since they were superstitious and would frequently hold witch burnings and kill off those they assumed were vampires or lycanthropes."

"And then what happened?" asked Raban.

"My mother grew more and more ill as her body changed to needing only blood and not what we would call normal food," replied Orlock. "The nuns would feed her the blood of animals, which did the trick, although not for long. My mother became more hostile as time wore on, and one day she escaped the convent. She attacked a home in a nearby village, draining the blood of the residents there.

"When the townsfolk heard of this, they chased her into the town church and set it on fire with her locked inside. I was told later by the sisters in the convent that it wasn't the flames that took her life but a fallen rafter. It pierced her heart and she died from that. I was only ten years old when she died."

"I'm sorry, Captain," murmured Raban, his eyes darting in shock.

"That was some two hundred years ago," said Orlock.

Raban abruptly stood up. "Captain!" he exclaimed. "So that would make you . . ."

"Yes," interrupted Orlock. "I'm old."

Raban paused and sat back down in the chair. "So what about you?" he asked. "What happened to you after that?"

"I grew up," replied Orlock. "I grew up just like any other child, although with a group of nuns rather than in a typical household, and when I started my life on the open sea, I discovered that my mother was the daughter of a marquis, a nobleman. That is where I took my first name of Marquis from.

"When I reached my full potential as a man, that is when the vampire genetics set in . . . and now here I stand today. I can't die and I am forced to watch generations grow up, grow old, and die around me. It is quite the curse, my dear Raban."

"I am sorry for you, Captain," whispered Raban. "I won't say a word to anyone . . . even unto death."

"Thank you," smiled Orlock. "It will be good for you to know that I have not fed on any human being in all these years. However, I am hoping that when we reach the next island there is animal food there for me in the wilderness. I am starving."

"I will help you, Captain," said Raban. "Now that I understand, I will help you find blood-filled game."

Suddenly, the entire ship rocked violently and shuddered. Orlock and Raban looked up, stunned at the jolt. Thunder began to rumble loudly and the two men swiftly stood, breathing heavily.

"The storm is upon us," murmured Orlock.

"What was that jolt?" exclaimed Raban.

"I am praying that we don't have company," grumbled Orlock as he stormed past the first mate and toward the door.

"Company?" asked Raban.

"These waters are known to contain a creature," said Orlock as he began to open the door. "And that is something I pray is not waiting for us outside."

The two men raced up onto the deck as a storm raged around the ship. Rain whipped their faces and the salt of the sea stung their eyes. Crewmen raced about the deck in a panic, screaming and shouting in fear. Orlock and Raban's eyes grew wide as a massive tentacle slithered across the deck. It was a deep red color and covered in slime.

Orlock ordered Raban to grab their swords from below deck as he ran to aid the men and get a better look at the creature that began to raise itself up on the side of the ship. As he reached the ship's railing, Orlock could see the large yellow eye of the creature.

"A giant octopus, Captain!" shouted a crewman to Orlock.

"The Kraken!" exclaimed Orlock. "Men, grab spears and swords!"

The men dashed about and grabbed instruments to fight off the creature's mighty tentacles. Raban rushed to Orlock's side and handed him his sword. The two men began to stab at the slimy mass of tentacles. The creature raised its head out of the raging water, exposing its razor-sharp beak. Crewmen swung their weapons at the beak as it snapped at them. One man was caught in the slithering grasp of a tentacle and hurled into the beast's gaping jaws.

Orlock dashed to the creature's side, where its glaring eye was exposed, and began to plunge his sword into it, over and over. The creature let out a penetrating screech, and its tentacles began to writhe and convulse violently.

"It's retreating!" shouted Orlock to the men as the tentacles began to coil on themselves.

The men watched as the mighty beast slowly slid back into the waves that surrounded the ship. The storm began to quiet as this happened, leaving the crew standing on the deck, drenched in water and shaking with fear.

Orlock placed his hand on a trembling Raban's shoulder.

"Let's pray that we get to the destination without any more mishaps," said Orlock quietly. "We should be there in a couple more days."

The first mate nodded in response, wiped his forehead with trembling fingers, and sighed.

The evening faded into the darkness of night, and the full moon rose above the ocean. The tide lapped at the shore with sparkling white flashes of light as moonbeams reflected on the waves. In the blackness of the cave, Audrelle could see her surroundings somewhat since the moon's light gave some visibility through the cave's opening. She sat on the cold floor with her head hung low, eyeing the shackles that were locked onto her wrists. They were cold and uncomfortable as they dug into her skin.

Audrelle pulled on the chains attached to the wall of the cave once more in half-hearted desperation before leaning back against the cave wall and sighing. With tear-stained cheeks, she looked over at the mouth of the cave and closed her eyes, listening to the ocean to try to relax. She began to feel awfully strange and uncomfortable as a sensation like burning fire raced through her veins.

Audrelle opened her eyes and looked down questioningly at her limbs, which began to tremble. "What's happening to me?" she asked herself, fear and tension rising inside her. She stood up quickly as the chains clanked beside her and looked down at her hands. The burning sensation grew more intolerable with each passing second. She felt her fingers begin to cramp.

To Audrelle's horror, her fingers began to grow longer! The color of the skin on her hands grew paler and more gray. The gray color began to spread like wildfire from her hands up her arms. Audrelle gasped in terror as the sensation inside her body reached her head, causing a tremendous headache that made her feel like she was going to lapse into unconsciousness. Her fingernails changed shape and turned into long, black talons, and her legs gave out from under her. A green fog appeared around her and began to envelop her limp legs.

When the fog cleared, Audrelle screamed. Where her legs used to be, there was now a long serpent's tail! Her spine began to stretch painfully, causing her to grow taller. The shackles and chains pulled tight against the cave wall as she grew. As the cave floor became smaller and smaller, the whole world became fuzzy and turned into what seemed like a dream.

Audrelle pulled on the shackles with as much force as she could muster. Her arms had grown much larger, which made the shackles unbearably tight. The chains began to give way from the rock and then snapped with a loud *pling*. With a tremendous effort, Audrelle managed to break the shackle bracelets from her wrists as well.

Upon freeing herself, Audrelle slithered toward the opening of the cave with incredible speed. When she came out into the moonlight, she could clearly see what had happened to her. She was now over fifteen feet tall, her skin had the look and texture of a reptilian gargoyle, her legs had grown into a huge snake tail, and her hair was as white as the moon's rays. As she stared out over the ocean, with eyes that were glossed over completely white, the urge to fly came over her.

With a convulsive jolt, massive black wings sprouted from between her shoulders and stretched themselves open. Audrelle raised herself up and, with fists clenched, let out a deep roar at the night sky. She began to flap her wings, churning up the sand beneath her in a cloud of debris, and soared off into the sky.

"She escaped," said the corpse guard to King Merlot the next morning.

"I cannot believe it," hissed Merlot, enraged. "Get your best men and find her! She could not have left the island. She would have had to fly for such a long time before she reached land on another island that she would have perished in the sea from exhaustion."

"Yes, my king," answered the guard. "If she is here, we will find her."

King Merlot leaned back on his throne and rubbed his eyes. "I can't believe she broke the chains," he said to himself. "She must be a lot stronger than I anticipated. If I can't find the princess and get her under my control, my entire plan will fail. This cannot happen!"

The village on the other side of the island woke up calmly as the sun began to peek over the tree line that enveloped it, and the villagers went about their daily duties. It was in one of the homes in the village that Audrelle awoke. She was confused and bewildered as she sat up in a small bed. She looked at her hands and touched her face. They weren't those of the serpent creature she had transformed into the night before.

Audrelle was in the home of an elderly woman. "Just relax, my dear," said the woman soothingly.

"Where am I?" asked Audrelle.

"You're in our village on the other side of the island," replied the woman. "You can call me Margaret. I'm an elder in this community."

"I had the strangest dream," murmured Audrelle as she moved over to sit on the edge of the bed.

"What was your dream about?" asked Margaret.

"I dreamed that I was locked in King Merlot's cave," said Audrelle. "And that I turned into some winged-serpent monster from a prophecy Merlot had told me about."

"It wasn't a dream," said Margaret as calmly as possible.

"What?" exclaimed the princess.

"You flew into our village last night," continued Margaret. "You scared several of the villagers, but I was able to calm them. I recognized the creature you were since I am a keeper of the tales, prophecies, and myths of the regional lands."

Audrelle's mouth fell open in shock. She tried to contain her overwhelming emotions as the previous day's memories flooded into her mind, but it only resulted in a breakdown. "What am I to do?" she wailed with her face in her hands. Tears streamed between her fingers. "I am a monster now!"

Margaret rushed to the side of the broken woman slouched on the edge of the bed. "It'll be okay," she soothed, rubbing Audrelle's back. "You didn't hurt anyone!"

Audrelle slowly looked up into the older woman's caring gaze. "I'm glad for that," she whimpered, sniffing. "I don't know what to do."

"According to the prophecy, you now have a great responsibility," said Margaret. "You now will help play a major role in the wicked King Merlot's takeover. It will be you who will help decide whether evil or goodness will rule in the end in our lands."

"I don't want that responsibility!" said Audrelle. She shook in fear. "I just want to go home!"

"My dear," continued Margaret, "the lands and the people who live in them are counting on you now. You're our princess, and one day you'll be our queen. Don't you want to help your people?"

Audrelle sat in silence and began to calm herself. "Yes," she whispered. "I would want that more than anything. I'm just so scared."

"I understand," said Margaret. "We believe in you. That's why last night, when you flew into our village from the skies, we were sure to keep you calm in your other state until the sun came up and you returned to your human form. We knew that it was the beginning of the long-awaited hope we seek."

"Thank you." Audrelle smiled and wiped her wet cheeks. "What will I have to do?"

"You'll have to defeat Merlot and Gorgomesh," answered the older woman. "When the time is right, Merlot and Gorgomesh will rise up to take over the lands. You will be there to stop his army, should you choose to do so. Merlot will try to sway you while you are in serpent form, and it will be difficult for you. It is said that help will come to you, although that part of the story is vague. We do not know the details about who or what will come to your aid. The village will fight back as best as they can against Merlot's undead army . . . but the only power great enough to destroy the final evil barrier—that is, Merlot and Gorgomesh the dragon—will be you."

"When will they strike?" asked Audrelle, slowly rising to her feet.

"Well," replied Margaret, "that is difficult to determine, although it will probably be during the time of the full moon when the power of the winged serpent is at its strongest. Merlot will want that more than anything—for you to be in your serpent form so he can try to sway you to his side. Otherwise, his power cannot reach its full potential."

"So I have a month until the next change?" continued Audrelle earnestly. "Merlot will be looking for me until then, I assume."

"Yes," answered Margaret. "You must hide in the village and surrounding forest to the best of your abilities during this time to avoid being caught and locked in Merlot's grasp. I imagine they are already out on the hunt for you now."

"Will the village help me?" asked Audrelle.

"Of course," replied Margaret. "We will do everything in our power to help you."

Audrelle sighed with relief at Margaret's kindness. "Thank you," she said. "I cannot thank you enough. I will do everything I can to do the right thing in the end for everyone."

Margaret smiled and walked over to a table on the other side of the room. "Now, dear, you must eat," she said, her tone becoming motherly. "Here, sit down and eat the porridge I made for breakfast."

Audrelle giggled and sat down at the table while Margaret went to the pot of food and scooped it into a bowl.

As Marquis Orlock's ship sailed over the calm morning sea, the sound of seagulls could be heard. Orlock walked to the bow of the ship and rubbed the sleep from his eyes while Raban joined him and stood by his side.

"Today is the day, correct?" asked Raban.

"We should be able to see the island at some point this morning," replied Orlock. "That is, if the storm didn't blow us off course too much."

Raban nodded in response. "Hopefully that won't be the case," he said. "What will be your first orders when we reach the island?"

"I don't have a clue at the moment," replied Orlock. "Although I do know that I will go ashore alone to scope out the island first and come back to the ship with orders after that."

"Are you sure that is wise, Captain?" asked Raban.

"It's my choice," replied Orlock. "After losing two men on this journey so far, I am not risking any more lives until I am certain what I am up against to fulfill the vision and destiny I received from myself and the oracle."

"I understand, Captain," said Raban quietly. "I will be sure to take care of the ship until your return."

"I know you will," said Orlock with a smile. He placed a hand on Raban's shoulder. "I'm not worried about that."

In the distance, the silhouette of land appeared. Orlock and Raban looked at each other.

"Land, Captain," said Raban.

"Yes, the island we seek," added Orlock. "Have the men prepare to cast anchor after sounding."

Raban nodded and left Orlock's side to carry out the order.

As the ship drew closer to the island, Orlock had it anchored in a cove that contained tall reef formations. The formations kept the ship out of sight from the shore, which was Orlock's intention to make their arrival unnoticeable to Merlot and his minions. He figured there wasn't much of a choice in their staying hidden should Gorgomesh the dragon spot the ship, but this option was better than nothing.

Orlock had the men lower him in a skiff from the ship, and he rowed the little craft into a secluded spot on the shore with plenty of tree cover. After hiding the skiff in some reeds and covering it with tall grasses, Orlock began the trek through the forest that lay ahead of him. "I hope I can find Merlot's castle or the princess soon," mumbled Orlock to himself. "It could take a while until I find someone or something that will give me a clue about where to go next."

He walked on for an hour or so until he came to the edge of the forest. A clearing lay ahead of him. It contained little homes and small buildings. "A village?" he asked himself.

"Maybe someone who lives here will know where I need to go."

Margaret, the village elder, walked over to a well at the edge of the village to fill a pail of water and saw the captain walk toward her from the forest's edge. After a moment of thought, her look of puzzlement turned into a grin. She filled the pail and quickly turned from the well and walked back to her home.

Audrelle, who was sitting by the fireplace doing some needlework, looked up as Margaret came into the room.

"Someone's coming!" said Margaret excitedly.

"Who?" asked Audrelle. She jumped up in fear. "Merlot? One of his guards?"

"No," replied Margaret, "I've never seen this man before."

"What should I do?" asked Audrelle earnestly. "Is he coming this way? Should I hide?"

"No," said Margaret. "If he comes to the door, just answer it."

"Why should I answer it?" asked Audrelle, annoyed.

"No more questions," answered the old woman. "Just do as I say, please."

Audrelle, puzzled, watched Margaret as she rushed out of the room and went to her bedroom and shut the door behind her. At that moment, a light knock came from the front door. Audrelle jolted at the sound and looked over at the door, trying not to pant in fear. "It's probably nothing to worry about," she whispered to herself. "Just listen to Margaret and answer the door."

She tiptoed to the door and jolted again as another knock sounded. "I'm coming," Audrelle said with a sigh. She opened the door to a crack and peered out. She saw Orlock standing in the doorway. He was shocked that someone finally answered the door.

"H-hello," stammered Orlock as Audrelle continued to peer through the crack in the door at him. "I am a traveler, and I was hoping someone here could help me?"

Audrelle slowly opened the door and stood with her hand on her cocked hip. She tried to act as nonchalantly as possible, but struggled to maintain her composure since she couldn't help but gawk at the man's long black hair and dark eyes. "How can I help you, sir?" she asked, trying not to bite her lip.

Orlock stood transfixed on her for a moment, admiring her long golden locks and big brown eyes. "I, um," he stuttered, "I have come to seek help in knowing where the castle of King Merlot is located?"

Audrelle's face fell when she heard Merlot's name. "What business do you have with Merlot?" she asked.

"It's a long story," replied Orlock. "Do you know the way to his castle? I need to find a princess he has captured."

Audrelle's eyes lit up with excitement. "Please, sir, come in and explain," she said with a smile.

At first Marquis Orlock was hesitant to reveal his vision, and his journey to the oracle, to the young woman who invited him into the abode, but as they began to make small talk and after he was given a hot cup of tea, he began to relax and told her everything. Audrelle listened intently and, as he spoke, she began to feel a warmth toward Orlock growing with every second. She tried to not be too forward with him, but the yearning to explain to him that she was the princess in his vision became almost unbearable. When the emotions grew too overwhelming for her, Audrelle walked over to a window with her back turned toward the man.

"Is everything all right?" asked Orlock.

"Yes," replied Audrelle with a sigh. "It's such a beautiful morning. Shall we go for a walk?"

"All right," said Orlock. "If I said anything that disturbed you, I'm sorry."

Audrelle turned toward Orlock and smiled. "No," she said. "It's nothing like that. I could really just use some fresh air. Want me to show you a beautiful place that I know of?"

"Sure," answered Orlock, still feeling as though he had said too much to her.

The two walked out the front door of the little house and into the village. Margaret carefully opened her bedroom door, crept to the front door, and smiled as she watched Audrelle and Orlock leaving the village together.

"So where are we going?" asked Orlock as Audrelle led him from the village and into the forest.

"It's a beautiful spot I found," replied Audrelle. "It has the greenest grass I've ever seen and fascinating rock formations. I think you'll find it interesting. I figured we could find a spot to sit down there and talk more."

Orlock shrugged in agreement. The forest canopied them from above, letting rays of sunlight stream down onto the mossy ground all around them. Audrelle took Orlock gently by the hand and led him into a clearing up ahead. Orlock at first felt awkward holding her hand, given that he hadn't held a fair maiden's hand in a good many years, but the warmth of her palm felt nice on his cold skin.

"You have cold skin," said Audrelle as they walked out into the clearing. "How could you be cold on such a warm day as this?"

"I-I have poor circulation sometimes," stammered Orlock, trying to hide the fact that he was a vampire. "It runs in my family."

"Oh, I see," said Audrelle sweetly as she pointed at the view before them.

The view contained a vast field of beautiful green grasses and rock formations that were unlike anything Orlock had ever seen before. The rocks twisted and spiraled toward the sky. Birds flitted among the formations and deer nibbled on the rich, green grass.

"Yes, you were right," said Orlock in awe. "It is a beautiful area."

"Too bad that just beyond the rock formations lies Merlot's castle," sighed

Audrelle, eyeing Orlock carefully. "I never want to go back there."

Orlock looked at Audrelle in surprise. "You mean—?" he started to say.

"Yes," interrupted Audrelle, her eyes locked onto Orlock's. "I am that princess you seek."

Orlock hesitated a moment as the flood of emotions he had kept pent up during his journey and since he had had the vision to seek out the oracle long before rushed to the forefront of his mind. "So you are the Princess Audrelle," he said, kissing her hand. "I am sorry for not showing more respect in the presence of royalty!"

Audrelle laughed at him. "None needed," she said. "I haven't been living like royalty for quite some time now. I went from my father's nice, warm kingdom to being captured by Gorgomesh the dragon and Merlot's corpse army, to Merlot's castle, to being locked up in a cave, then to the village where I've been hiding."

"I am sorry, my princess," said Orlock, bowing.

"You may call me by my name, kind sir," laughed Audrelle. "What may I call you?"

"My name is Marquis Orlock," he answered. "You may call me whatever you wish."

"I'll just call you Mark," said Audrelle. "Is that okay?"

Orlock paused in thought for a moment. "Hmm," he said, rubbing his chin. "Mark . . . not bad."

Audrelle grinned and walked closer to him. "So you are the one who is to help me," she whispered.

"I guess so." Orlock smiled.

"So let's take some time here," said Audrelle, "to get to know each other better. Then we will go back into the village and see Margaret the elder so she can give us some words of wisdom as to how we might stop Merlot and Gorgomesh before it's too late."

"Yes, princess," stammered Orlock nervously.

"Audrelle," she corrected with a playful glint in her eyes.

"Yes," said Orlock. He paused and then corrected himself. "Audrelle."

Later that evening, back in the village, Audrelle and Orlock sat at the dinner table with Margaret.

"So the things you said concerning the legend and prophecy are coming to fruition," said Audrelle to Margaret.

Margaret took a bite of her food. "I'm amazed at how fast all these things are falling into place," she said as she turned to Orlock.

"It definitely all adds up," said Orlock to Margaret. "From my receiving that map in the Bermuda Triangle, to my vision, to my seeing the oracle. Then learning all that happened with Audrelle and Merlot, and the specifics told to me by the oracle concerning them and my needing to help, all add up to this prophecy you told Audrelle."

"And it aligns with the things I heard Merlot say about his plans with Gorgomesh," chimed in Audrelle. "Definitely none of this is a coincidence."

Margaret nodded in agreement at both of them. "Time is of the essence," she said. "Merlot must have his army out looking for Audrelle, and they more than likely are getting close. After all, this island isn't very big. Although the mountain region that lies between the village and Merlot's castle could detain them for a little while, we must be ready for them."

"I could leave tonight," said Orlock, "and head back to my ship and get my men in here. The ship is anchored on this side of the island in a cove."

"That would help," said Margaret. "The village has been preparing for just such an occasion for a long time now, so if forces are joined, we will have a fairly good defense set up."

"Fairly good?" asked Audrelle.

"None of the villagers, and I imagine Orlock's crew, are truly prepared to fight an undead army, the mighty dragon Gorgomesh, and the black magic of Merlot," replied Margaret.

"My men may not have much experience in fighting black magic," said Orlock, "but they have overcome many creatures on our voyages. Creatures that most thought were merely legends of mythology."

"That's good to know," smiled Margaret. "The undead army can't be killed. But they can be destroyed in battle if they are rendered helpless in movement."

"So chop off the heads and limbs," declared Audrelle to Orlock with a glint of humor in her eyes.

Orlock chuckled at the princess's morbid statement. "I shall leave here shortly then," he said, "and get my men in here."

The three at the table finished their meal and cleaned up afterward. When Orlock departed, after Audrelle planted a kiss on his cheek, he ran into the dark forest toward the cove where his ship was anchored.

When Orlock arrived at the ship, he awoke Raban, who was sleeping in his cabin. "Wake up, mate," whispered Orlock to a befuddled Raban. "We need to get the men to the village. A war is about to start."

Raban jumped up and rubbed his forehead. "Yes, Captain," he answered. "Should we leave someone at the ship to keep watch?"

"Of course," replied Orlock. "Keep three men here to take care of the ship, and I'll give them the orders as to their plan of action should something come up and tell them to signal if anything happens while we are away."

Raban nodded in agreement, and the two men rushed throughout the rest of the ship and woke the others.

"Men, listen up!" shouted Orlock to the crew on the deck as he stood before them all. "This army you may have to fight is undead. They cannot be killed."

"Then what's the point, Captain?" asked a crew member. "I don't want to be part of some suicide mission!"

As other crew members shouted in agreement, Orlock looked over at a fearful Raban. "Silence!" continued Orlock. "They cannot be killed. However, if you can render them useless, you will be the victor!"

"Chop off the heads and limbs," added Raban. "If they can't move, then they are nothing but a bunch of bones!"

Orlock grinned in approval at Raban. The crew fell silent and then agreed with the captain and first mate.

Once Orlock had the majority of his crew prepared for battle, they all left the ship as quickly and silently as possible. As they entered the forest and began heading toward the village, with only the light of the moon as a lamp, they heard an unearthly screech that pierced the air ahead of them. They all stopped dead in their tracks.

"What in heaven's name was that, Captain?" whispered Raban to Orlock urgently.

"Gorgomesh," growled Orlock. "The sound came from the area in which we are headed . . . the village. We need to move fast!"

The captain waved the men forward, and they all moved ahead with a fierce determination. Their metal weapons and what little armor they had on hand clanked in the silence of the black trees.

"There is the village," said Orlock to everyone when the trees began to clear ahead of them.

The sight that met them when they came out of the forest was terrifying. The village was glowing orange, and plumes of smoke emanated from spots within it. The cries of peasant warriors and the screeches of Merlot's corpse army echoed all around. Orlock ordered his men to charge.

What followed was a battle of terrific proportions. Orlock's crew swung their swords and spears at the invading army of rotting corpse warriors. Metal clanked and screeched as the two armies fell upon each other. The crew decapitated the undead warriors, hacked off limbs, and did everything they could to obey the captain's orders.

"Raban!" shouted Orlock to the first mate as he drove off a warrior with a swing of his sword. "I'm going to Margaret's! I need to make sure they are safe!"

"Aye, aye, Captain," shouted Raban while he crossed swords with an undead soldier and stared into the hollow sockets of its skeletal face.

Orlock rushed over to Margaret's house and, to his horror, found it in flames. "Audrelle!" screamed Orlock. "Margaret!"

When he reached the doorway of the house, Orlock thrust himself into the flame-filled opening. He looked around the main room, which hadn't been taken over completely by the fire, and saw the body of Margaret lying on the floor. He rushed over to the old woman and saw that she was still breathing. Orlock picked her up, carried her into the open air outside, and set her down safely away from the inferno.

"Audrelle." Margaret coughed and wheezed.

"Where is she?" asked Orlock.

"Merlot and his first guard," replied Margaret. She winced. "They came in not long after you left for your ship. They took her. Then Gorgomesh came and started setting the village on fire."

"Do you know if they took her back to his castle?" asked Orlock.

"Most likely," replied Margaret. "Leave me and go save her."

"I'm not leaving you," said Orlock sternly. "I'll have you brought to my ship until this is over."

Raban ran up to the kneeling Orlock, who was holding Margaret in his arms. "Captain," he said, "the corpse army is retreating—what's left of it. What are your orders?"

"Take this woman back to the safety of the ship," ordered Orlock. "Have the rest of the crew douse the fires in the village and then return to the ship until further orders."

"Aye, aye, Captain," answered Raban, carefully picking up the weakened Margaret.

"Thank you, Raban," said Orlock as the first mate turned to leave.

Raban turned his head and nodded. "We are with you all the way, Captain," he said with a grin.

Once Orlock's crew had put out the fires in the village, they all went back to the ship and waited patiently while Margaret was attended to. In the meantime, Marquis Orlock began his journey toward Merlot's castle. He followed the direction in which Audrelle had pointed when they were in that beautiful area the day before. After all his experiences in traveling over rough terrain on his voyages, Orlock found the mountainous region that lay between the village and Merlot's castle to be quite easy in comparison.

It wasn't long before Orlock saw the outline of the decrepit castle on top of the foothill lit from behind by the rays of the rising sun. He stopped for a brief rest when he reached the base of the mountain. He saw the beach on one side of the mountain, the ocean waves lapping it. On the other, the rocky region that led to the village stretched before him.

"I hope I will get to her in time," muttered Orlock to himself, thinking of Audrelle and missing her adorable little smile. "I hope she is okay." He tried to not be sentimental at a time like this—too much was at stake, and he needed to move forward—but he couldn't help but feel soft inside when he had been so hard of heart for so long. These emotions confused him, and he tried to fight them off, but he knew deep down that he simply could not. With a sigh and a stretch, he stood up and started the trek up the path carved into the side of the hill toward the castle.

Audrelle sat on her knees, hands bound behind her, on the floor of Merlot's throne chamber. Her hair covered her face as she glared through the golden locks at the wizard king, who stood before her in front of his throne.

"Your little escape didn't last very long, princess," sneered Merlot. "The time is coming for me to fulfill my destiny!"

"You'll never get away with this," murmured Audrelle defiantly.

"Such optimism," retorted Merlot with a chuckle. "You need to understand something, princess."

"What is that?" asked Audrelle, sullenly pulling at the rope that bound her wrists.

"That the cards are stacked against you," replied Merlot. "Or should I say against your beliefs. Evil will win in this case. You have no one here to save you, the village is burned, and I'm still on track to fulfill my destiny and seize power. Why do you persist in trying to defy me? After all, you'll gain power yourself only by joining forces with me."

"I will never join forces with a snake like you," snarled Audrelle.

"Forgive my forwardness, princess," said Merlot. A sly smile crossed his lips. "But it is *you* who is the snake. Or should I say, an actual snake."

"I was cursed with that because of *you*," hissed Audrelle. "You and your evil practices. I wanted nothing to do with any of it!"

"It's all part of the prophecy," snickered Merlot. "Now, very soon, Gorgomesh the dragon will be here and I will bring all the forces of my powers to the front and begin my reign of all the lands."

"You can't do it without me," said Audrelle. "Not when I'm in this form. So I will say that you won't be able to bring your plan to fruition. You will not sway me to join you."

Merlot shot a lightning bolt at the princess from his finger. Audrelle screeched as it hit her body and sent her reeling onto her back. She lay there panting from the shock but bit her lip and managed to shakily get back onto her knees. Merlot began to laugh, his bloodshot eyes glinting with crazed excitement. He shot another bolt at her, then another, and another. Each bolt struck Audrelle, leaving her writhing on the floor in pain.

"It'll only be a little while," shouted Merlot, "and you will see things my way!"

"I hate you!" hissed Audrelle, wincing in pain.

Merlot continued to hit Audrelle with his bolts until her eyes filled with rage. She wanted to destroy this wicked man but also began to feel as if she was falling into a deep sleep. "No!" she exclaimed as her eyes glossed over and turned white.

Merlot smiled with pleasure as he watched Audrelle begin to change into the winged serpent. "You see," he said, "the moon may not be full at the moment, but I have the ability to turn you if I can make you mad enough!"

Audrelle convulsed and then snapped the rope that bound her hands. She writhed around as her legs became a serpent's tail and her body grew larger. Merlot looked toward a big window in the chamber and watched the sun disappear behind black storm clouds. He pointed his finger toward the window and shot a bolt of green, glowing energy into the clouds beyond. Thunder and lightning crashed while the black clouds began to pulse with a glowing, green light.

Down the mountainside on the path, Marquis Orlock watched in fear as the sudden storm took over the skies. "Merlot is starting his plan," he said to himself. "I must hurry!"

At that moment, the thundering roar of Gorgomesh shook the skies. Orlock watched as the beast came into view, flying down from the skies toward the castle. The flapping of his wings made the ground tremble, and Orlock rushed up to the side of the castle and out of sight of the creature as it came in for a landing.

"Gorgomesh is here!" exclaimed Merlot to Audrelle, who now stood before him in winged-serpent form. "I told you! I will be the victor!"

The winged serpent looked down at the king beneath her. Thoughts of wanting to destroy him and confused thoughts of power and victory swirled around in her mind. She clutched her head in agony.

Orlock ran up to a door on the side of the castle and struck the padlock with his sword. The lock fell to the ground and the door swung open. He rushed into the dark castle and followed the sounds that were now emanating from the court chamber.

Gorgomesh crawled onto the roof of the castle and roared into the thundering skies above him while the flashes of green lighting intensified. Merlot stared up into the white eyes of Audrelle. "Once the storm I've started reaches its full potential, Gorgomesh will take in the powers emanating from it. At that moment, I will be one with the dragon and we will bring our powers together. You will be the final part of this unholy trinity!"

Audrelle looked from the window, where she could hear Gorgomesh roaring, to the wizard king beneath her. She wanted to scream and strike but found that her throat was in knots and that her arms were frozen and shaking. Just then, Marquis Orlock burst into the chamber.

Orlock stood with his sword leveled at Merlot, who stood between him and Audrelle. The winged serpent hissed in contempt and defiance at the sword pointed toward her and Merlot.

"You are above this!" shouted Orlock to the princess. "You don't have to be the slave of this man you think is your master!"

At first Audrelle's white eyes flashed with a fiery anger at Orlock, but as they darted from Orlock to Merlot, a great confusion came over her again. On the surface, Audrelle began to feel the instinct to protect the cloaked figure standing in front of her, with his back toward her, and to destroy the man with the drawn sword, but deep inside she felt the urge to destroy Merlot and help the man she had fallen in love with. These intense emotions battled within her, but then evil began to be overtaken by love.

"I can see that you're torn!" shouted Orlock. "Don't let the power of this man consume you, princess!"

"Hold your tongue!" hissed Merlot. "She is in my realm now! She is part of my alliance! She is part of my destiny!"

Audrelle looked down at Merlot as he said these things and then looked up at Orlock. Her eyes began to water, and her snarling lips began to tremble. Orlock looked deep into the winged-serpent princess's eyes, his brow furrowed. Merlot had been watching them with clenched teeth. His face fell as he witnessed the interaction between the two beings he was sandwiched between.

Silence descended on them. Only the sound of the three figures breathing could be heard.

"It's over for you," whispered Merlot to Orlock.

Audrelle snarled and reared up behind Merlot. She struck the evil king, and the blow sent him flying into a stone pillar across the room with a loud thud. Orlock reeled around and rushed toward the fallen king, who lay panting on the ground. Audrelle hissed and slithered past Orlock to Merlot. She picked up the king by the throat and lifted him toward her snarling face, ready to end his life right there. Merlot, shaking his head in a daze, came to and shot a bolt of lightning out of his fingers and into Audrelle's forehead. The winged serpent screeched as she dropped Merlot and gripped her head in pain. Orlock struck Merlot from behind with his sword, the blade sliding deep into the king's back and out the front of his stomach.

"My destiny!" screamed Merlot. He hunched over and fell to his knees. "This is not how things were supposed to happen!"

"It's over for *you*, my dear king," muttered Orlock, pulling the sword out of Merlot.

Just then the entire room began to quake. Audrelle and Orlock looked up in surprise at the sudden tremors. "We need to get out of here," said Orlock.

Audrelle nodded in understanding and grabbed Orlock as the walls of the chamber began to crumble. She stretched her wings and rose up into the air toward a large hole that appeared as the walls fell apart, exposing the thundering night sky outside the castle.

Merlot, greatly weakened, shakily rose to his feet and stumbled toward the opening the other two had escaped out of. "You will not win," he said, blood seeping from his mouth "I will take over everything, and the world will grovel at my feet!"

As Audrelle cleared the castle, holding Orlock firmly in her arm, Gorgomesh came swooping by and sent them spiraling through the air, out of control. The dragon landed next to the crumbling castle and roared, flames spewing out of his mouth.

"Merlot must be dying," said Orlock to Audrelle. "That is why the castle is falling apart and Gorgomesh seems to be panicking." Audrelle nodded in agreement.

Audrelle landed on the beach at the base of the mountain. She set Orlock down, and the two looked up at the castle where Gorgomesh continued to roar and rage and spout flames from his mouth.

"We need to destroy Gorgomesh," continued Orlock. "He is the last thing that needs to be defeated to end Merlot's reign of terror!"

Audrelle picked Orlock back up and the two flew up the mountainside and toward Gorgomesh. Orlock readied his sword to strike the dragon in the heart—which he'd do if he could get close enough and if Audrelle could help him do so.

From the opening of the crumbling castle, Merlot peered out and looked upon Gorgomesh. The dragon looked down at the wounded king in desperation. Merlot locked eyes with the creature, and for a brief moment, care-filled understanding passed between them. Gorgomesh knew their plan was beginning to crumble, so in one last fit of rage he roared again and looked at the winged serpent and sea captain as they barreled toward him from the skies. The dragon sent a wall of flames soaring at the two as they neared him.

Audrelle dodged the fireball and swooped down and around the base of the castle. Gorgomesh lifted his wings as the castle roof began to collapse and turned in fear toward Merlot. The evil king looked up in shock at the debris that was hurtling down toward him.

Audrelle and Orlock swiftly appeared to the right of Gorgomesh, swooping down for the kill. Orlock plunged his sword deep into the creature's chest. Gorgomesh screeched in agony as he reeled backward into the side of the castle. His massive body came down with the crumbling stone and landed on Merlot. The king was immediately crushed to death.

The entire mountain went up in a burst of green smoke and flames as the evil powers of Merlot and the prophecy began to dissipate. Gorgomesh let out one last roar as he lay dying in the ruins of the castle and as it completely collapsed on top of him.

Audrelle flew as fast as she could from the chaos of the site. As she did so, however, Orlock began to slip out of the crook of her arm. In an instant, he fell from her arm and plummeted toward the ocean below them. Realizing what had just happened, Audrelle stopped in shock and swooped down to catch the man before he hit the water. She managed to catch the helpless Orlock just as they both splashed down into the sea.

The storm quieted and the clouds cleared while the remainder of the green flames and lightning disappeared into the air. The charred remains of Merlot's mountaintop castle were all that stood. From the sea below, Marquis Orlock and the winged-serpent princess washed up onto the beach. The winged serpent held Orlock tightly in her arms, where he lay, panting. She released him as they lay there on the sand, staring up into the blue sky and sunlight that had reappeared. Orlock looked over at the large serpentine body of Audrelle, who lay with her wings sprawled out on the sand, and he sighed in relief that they were still alive.

"Thank you, princess," he whispered.

Audrelle was breathing heavily. Something mysterious had begun to happen. A slew of twinkling white lights appeared that swirled around her body. Her serpent tail morphed back into her human legs, her wings disappeared into the sand, and her body shrank back down to its normal size.

Orlock smiled at Audrelle as she sat up and pushed her hair from her face. "I'm cured?" she asked herself, staring down at her hands.

"The spell is broken," said Orlock. "You determined which way the prophecy was to go, and that was for good, and now you are no longer a winged serpent. You are the princess you started out to be—good—and your father's kingdom is safe now."

Audrelle looked over her shoulder excitedly at Orlock, who lay flat on his back on the beach and was beginning to groan. "I'm getting too old for this, I think," he muttered as he tried to sit up.

Audrelle leapt from where she sat, embraced Orlock, and kissed him passionately. Orlock at first was stunned but then decided to join in enthusiastically. After all, they were destined for each other.

They were sitting there on the beach, staring deeply into each other's eyes, when the boom of a cannon sounded from the sea. They both looked up, shocked at the noise, but relaxed when they realized it was Orlock's ship coming around the side of the island.

"My ship," said Orlock to Audrelle. "I'm glad to see her again. I can now take you back to your father's kingdom."

Audrelle gasped in excitement, but then her face fell.

"What's the matter?" asked Orlock.

"Margaret," replied Audrelle. "She must have been killed in the attack on the village. If she wasn't, I would have liked to have said goodbye to her."

"You will," smiled Orlock. "We got her safely out of the village during the attack, and my men doused the flames afterward."

Audrelle embraced Orlock with tears welling in her eyes. "I love you," she said.

Orlock paused for a moment in disbelief at what Audrelle had said. "I love you too," he whispered.

The ship anchored close to the shore, and Raban sent a skiff out to retrieve Orlock and Audrelle from the beach. When they had boarded, Orlock embraced Raban and praised the men for their bravery and victory. Audrelle was pleased to see that Margaret was all right, and she thanked her for all her kindness and help.

Orlock, Audrelle, and Raban took Margaret back to her village. The villagers had already begun to rebuild their damaged dwellings and were excited to see that Margaret was alive and well.

"Now that the reign of Merlot is over," said Margaret, looking at Audrelle and Orlock, "we don't have a king or queen."

"Maybe," said Audrelle, placing a finger to her mouth and glancing over at Orlock. "Just maybe . . ."

Marquis Orlock shook his head and rolled his eyes. "Oh brother," he said. "You don't mean . . .?"

Audrelle smiled and then giggled playfully. "We will get back to my father's kingdom and let him know the situation on the island," she said, turning from Orlock to Margaret. "I am sure things will work out just fine for the future of this land."

Raban patted Orlock on the back and winked at him. Orlock playfully shrugged at him in response. Audrelle happily slipped an arm around Orlock's waist. The villagers began to shout and cheer: "Hail to Queen Audrelle! Hail to King Orlock! Our island is victorious!"

And they lived happily ever after . . .

THE END

If you enjoyed this story, check out the other books available from Ray Thorne!

Dr. Andromeda Fallout

Dr. Andromeda Fallout Part 2

Please visit us at

www.raythornebooks.com

Thank you, and happy reading!